Table of Contents

Copyright © 2006 School Specialty Publishing. Published by Brighter Child®, an imprint of School Specialty Publishing, a member of the School Specialty Family.

Send all inquiries to:
School Specialty Publishing
8720 Orion Place
Columbus, OH 43240-2111

ISBN 0-7696-7661-8

2 3 4 5 6 7 8 9 10 WAL 09 08 07

Name ______________________

Name, Address, Phone

This book belongs to

______________________.

I live at

______________________.

The city I live in is

______________________.

The state I live in is

______________________.

My phone number is

______________________.

Short Vowels

Vowels are the letters **a**, **e**, **i**, **o** and **u**. Short **a** is the sound you hear in **ant**. Short **e** is the sound you hear in **elephant**. Short **i** is the sound you hear in **igloo**. Short **o** is the sound you hear in **octopus**. Short **u** is the sound you hear in **umbrella**.

Directions: Say the short vowel sound at the beginning of each row. Say the name of each picture. Then color the pictures which have the same short vowel sounds as that letter.

Short Vowel Sounds

Directions: In each box are three pictures. The words that name the pictures have missing letters. Write **a, e, i, o** or **u** to finish the words.

p _e_ n

p _i_ n

p _o_ n

b _u_ g

b _e_ g

b _u_ g

c _u_ t

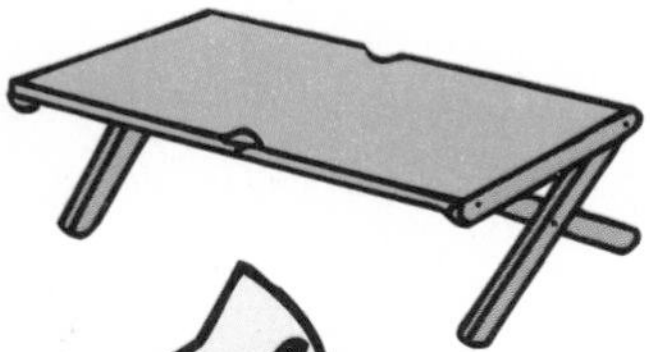

c _a_ t

c _u_ t

h _u_ t

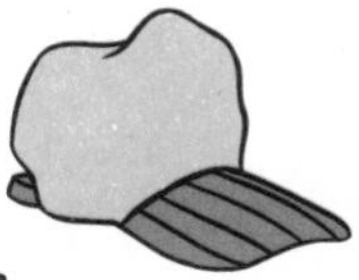

h _a_ t

h _o_ t

Long Vowels

Vowels are the letters **a**, **e**, **i**, **o** and **u**. Long vowel sounds say their own names. Long **a** is the sound you hear in **hay**. Long **e** is the sound you hear in **me**. Long **i** is the sound you hear in **pie**. Long **o** is the sound you hear in **no**. Long **u** is the sound you hear in **cute**.

Directions: Say the long vowel sound at the beginning of each row. Say the name of each picture. Color the pictures in each row that have the same long vowel sound as that letter.

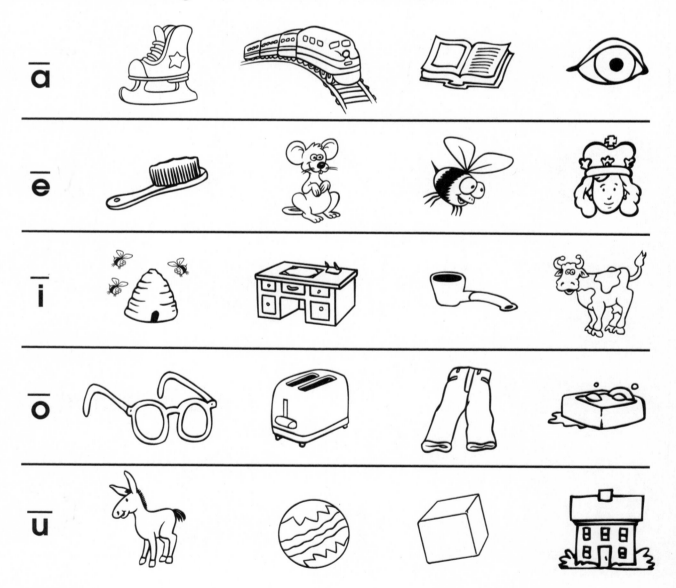

Long Vowel Sounds

Directions: Write **a, e, i, o** or **u** in each blank to finish the word. Draw a line from the word to the picture.

c ___ ke

r ___ se

k ___ te

f ___ t

m ___ le

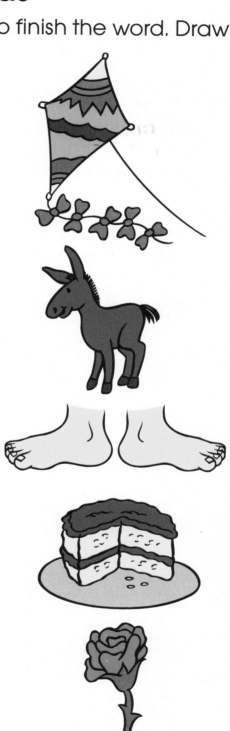

Consonant Blends

Consonant blends are two or more consonant sounds together in a word. The blend is made by combining the consonant sounds.

Example: floor

Directions: The name of each picture begins with a **blend**. Circle the beginning blend for each picture.

bl   fl   cl

cl   fl   gl

fl   bl   pl

fl   cl   gl

pl   gl   cl

gl   fl   sl

gl   fl   cl

sl   fl   cl

cl   gl   sl

Name ______________________________

Consonant Blends

Directions: The beginning blend for each word is missing. Fill in the correct blend to finish the word. Draw a line from the word to the picture.

_____ ain

_____ og

_____ ab

_____ um

_____ ush

_____ esent

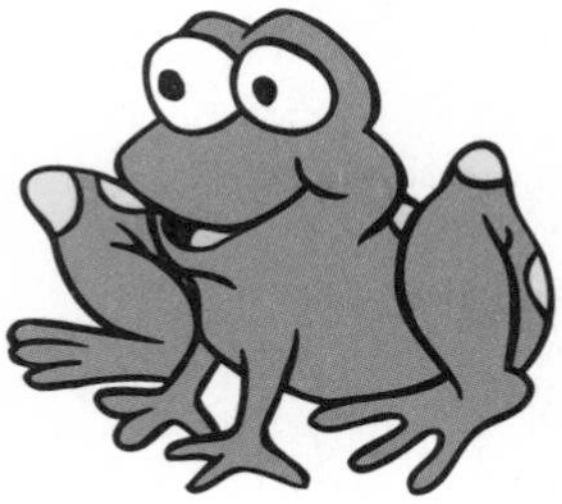

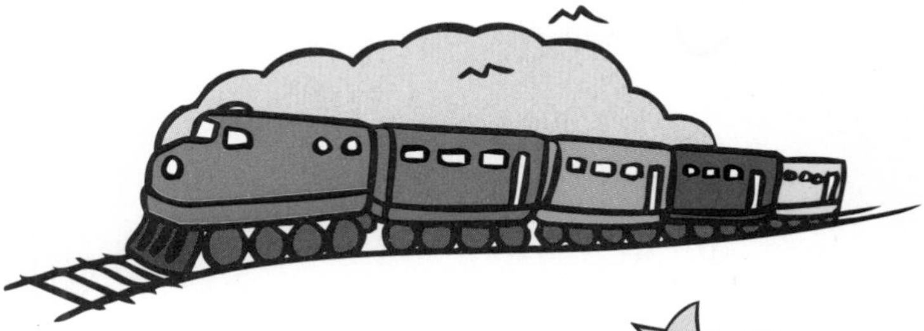

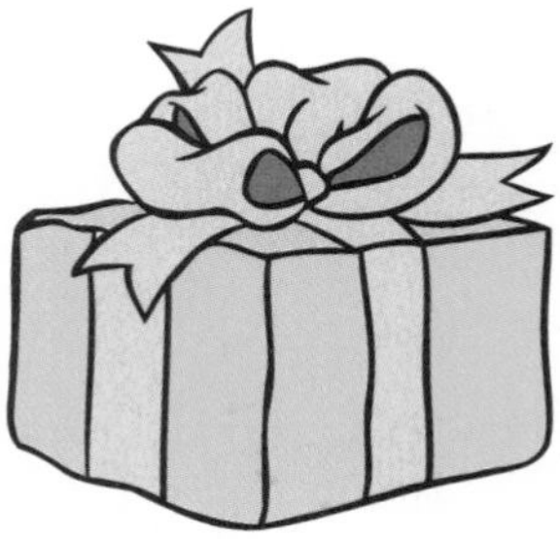

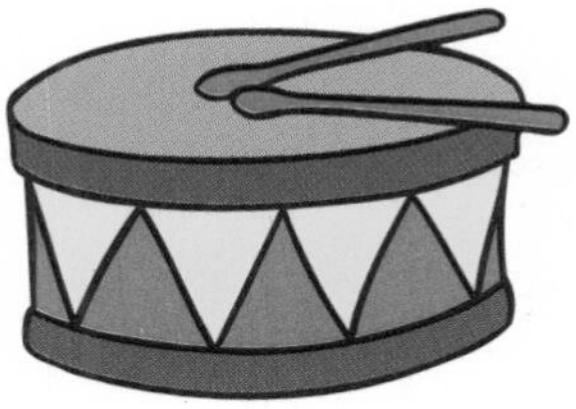

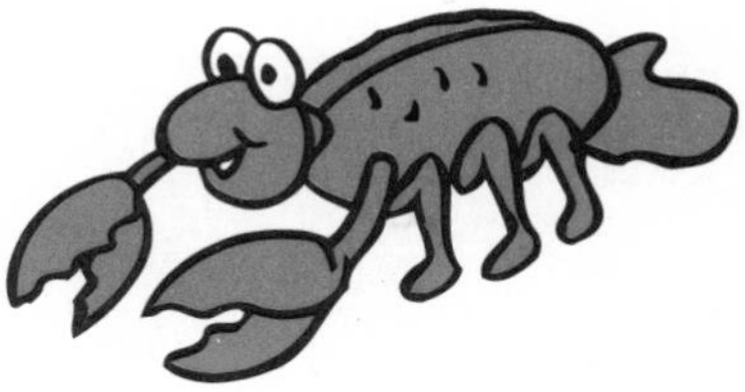

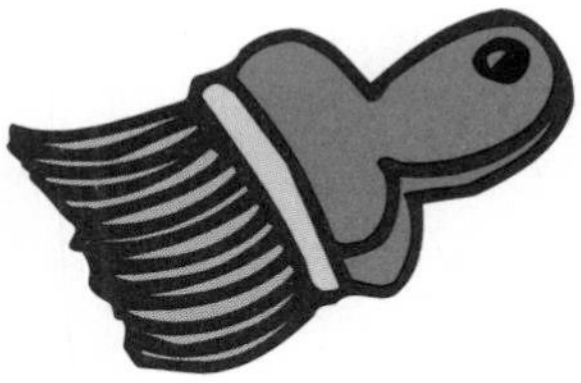

Compound Words

Compound words are two words that are put together to make one new word.

Directions: Look at the pictures and the two words that are next to each other. Put the words together to make a new word. Write the new word.

Example:

 +  =

house   boat

houseboat

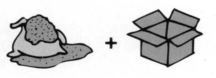 =

side   walk

_____

 =

lip   stick

_____

 =

sand   box

_____

 + =

lunch   box

_____

Compound Words

Directions: Circle the compound word which completes each sentence. Write each word on the lines.

1. The _____ brings us letters.

         mailman   snowman

2. A _____ grows tall.

    sunlight   sunflower

3. The snow falls _____.

    outside   inside

4. A _____ fell on my head.

    raindrop   rainbow

5. I put the letter in a _____.

    mailbox   shoebox

Riddles

Directions: Write a word from the box to answer each riddle.

| ice cream | book | chair | sun |

There are many words in me.
I am fun to read.
What am I?

I am soft and yellow.
You can sit on me.
What am I?

- -

I am in the sky in the day.
I am hot. I am yellow.
What am I?

I am cold. I am sweet.
You like to eat me.
What am I?

- -

Picture Clues

Directions: Read the sentence. Circle the word that makes sense. Use the picture clues to help you. Then write the word.

I ride on a
bike   hike

I ride on a
train   tree

I ride in a
car   can

I ride on a
bus   bug

I ride in a
jar   jet

I ride in a
took   truck

Comprehension

Directions: Look at the picture. Write the words from the box to finish the sentences.

frog	log	bird	fish	ducks

The _____ can jump.

The turtle is on a _____ .

A _____ is in the tree.

The boy wants a _____ .

I see three _____ .

Following Directions: Color the Path

Directions: Color the path the girl should take to go home. Use the sentences to help you.

1. Go to the school and turn left.
2. At the end of the street, turn right.
3. Walk past the park and turn right.
4. After you pass the pool, turn right.

Classifying

Directions: Classifying is sorting things into groups. Draw a circle around the pictures that answer the question.

What Can Swim?

What Can Fly?

16

Sequencing: Raking Leaves

Directions: Write a number in each box to show the order of the story.

17 *Basic Skills Helpers: Grade 1*

Comprehension

Directions: Read the story. Write the words from the story that complete each sentence.

Jane and Bill like to play in the rain. They take off their shoes and socks.
They splash in the puddles.
It feels cold!
It is fun to splash!

_____

- -

Jane and Bill like to _____.

_____

- -

They take off their _____.

_____

- -

They splash in _____.

Do you like to splash in puddles?   Yes   No

Name_____

Comprehension: Growing Flowers

Directions: Read about flowers. Then write the answers.

Some flowers grow in pots. Many flowers grow in flower beds. Others grow beside the road. Flowers begin from seeds. They grow into small buds. Then they open wide and bloom. Flowers are pretty!

1. Name two places flowers grow.

_____

- -

_____

- -

2. Flowers begin from _____.

3. Then flowers grow into small _____.

4. Flowers then open wide and _____.

Comprehension: Tigers

Directions: Read about tigers. Then write the answers.

Tigers sleep during the day. They hunt at night. Tigers eat meat. They hunt deer. They like to eat wild pigs. If they cannot find meat, tigers will eat fish.

1. When do tigers sleep?

_____

- -

2. Name two things tigers eat.

- -

- -

- -

3. When do tigers hunt?

20

Following Directions: Tiger Puzzle

Directions: Read the story about tigers again. Then complete the puzzle.

Across:

1. When tigers cannot get meat, they eat_____ .

3. The food tigers like best is _____ .

4. Tigers like to eat this meat: wild _____ .

Down:

2. Tigers do this during the day.

     Basic Skills Helpers: Grade 1

Following Directions: Draw a Tiger

Directions: Follow directions to complete the picture of the tiger.

1. Draw black stripes on the tiger's body and tail.

2. Color the tiger's tongue red.

3. Draw claws on the feet.

4. Draw a black nose and two black eyes on the tiger's face.

5. Color the rest of the tiger orange.

6. Draw tall, green grass for the tiger to sleep in.

22

Predicting: Story Ending

Directions: Read the story. Draw a picture in the last box to complete the story.

That's my ball.

I got it first.

It's mine!

Making Inferences: Feelings

Directions: Read each story. Choose a word from the box to show how each person feels.

happy	excited	sad	mad

1. Andy and Sam were best friends. Sam and his family moved far away. How does Sam feel?

   _____

   - - - - - - - - - - - - - - - -

   _____

2. Deana could not sleep. It was the night before her birthday party. How does Deana feel?

   _____

   - - - - - - - - - - - - - - - -

   _____

3. Jacob let his baby brother play with his teddy bear. His brother lost the bear. How does Jacob feel?

   _____

   - - - - - - - - - - - - - - - -

   _____

4. Kia picked flowers for her mom. Her mom smiled when she got them. How does Kia feel?

   _____

   - - - - - - - - - - - - - - - -

   _____

Nouns

A noun is a word that names a person, place or thing. When you read a sentence, the noun is what the sentence is about.

Directions: Complete each sentence with a noun.

The _____ is fat.

My _____ is blue.

The _____ has apples.

The _____ is hot.

Name ____________________

Nouns

Directions: Write these naming words in the correct box.

store	zoo	child	baby	teacher	table
cat	park	gym	woman	sock	horse

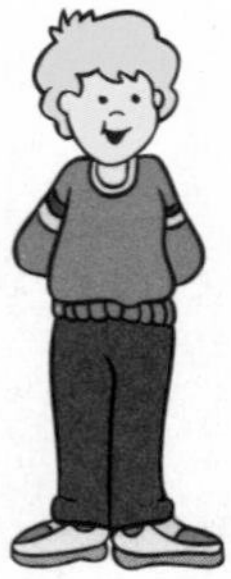

Person

____________________ ____________________

____________________ ____________________

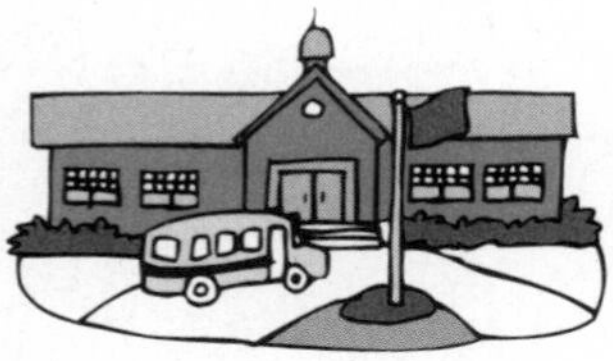

Place

____________________ ____________________

____________________ ____________________

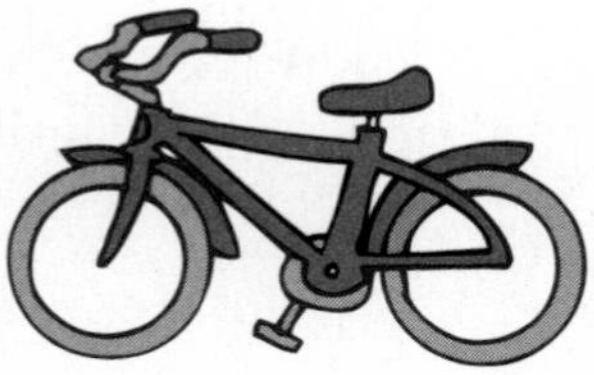

Thing

____________________ ____________________

____________________ ____________________

Name _____

Verbs

Verbs are words that tell what a person or a thing can do.

Example: The girl pats the dog.
The word **pats** is the verb. It shows action.

Directions: Draw a line between the verbs and the pictures that show the action.

   eat

                                                            run

   sleep

   swim

   sing

   hop

Verbs

Directions:
Look at the picture and read the words. Write an action word in each sentence below.

1. The two boys like to _____ together.

2. The children _____ the soccer ball.

3. Some children like to _____ on the swing.

4. The girl can _____ very fast.

5. The teacher _____ the bell.

28

Words That Describe

Describing words tell us more about a person, place or thing.

Directions: Read the words in the box. Choose the word that describes the picture. Write it next to the picture.

happy	round	sick	cold	long

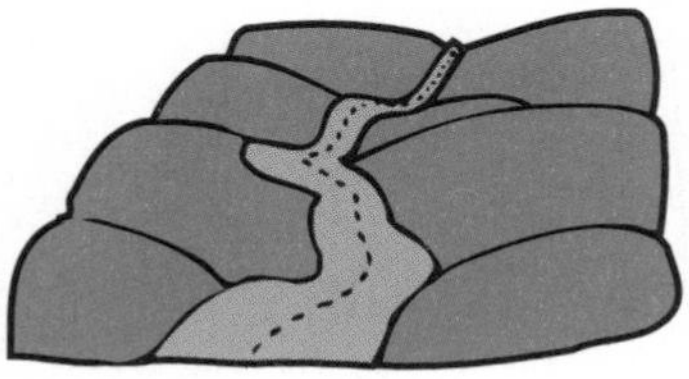

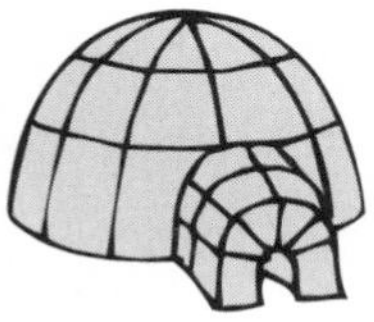

Words That Describe

Directions: Circle the describing word in each sentence. Draw a line from the sentence to the picture.

1. The hungry dog is eating.

2. The tiny bird is flying.

3. Horses have long legs.

4. She is a fast runner.

5. The little boy was lost.

Synonyms

Synonyms are words that mean almost the same thing. **Start** and **begin** are synonyms.

Directions: Find the synonyms that describe each picture. Write the words in the boxes below the picture.

small   funny   large   sad   silly   little   big   unhappy

31

Antonyms

Antonyms are words that are opposites. **Hot** and **cold** are antonyms.
Directions: Draw a line between the antonyms.

closed

below

full

empty

above

old

new

open

Homophones

Homophones are words that **sound** the same but are spelled differently and mean something different. **Blew** and **blue** are homophones.

Directions: Look at the word pairs. Choose the word that describes the picture. Write the word on the line next to the picture.

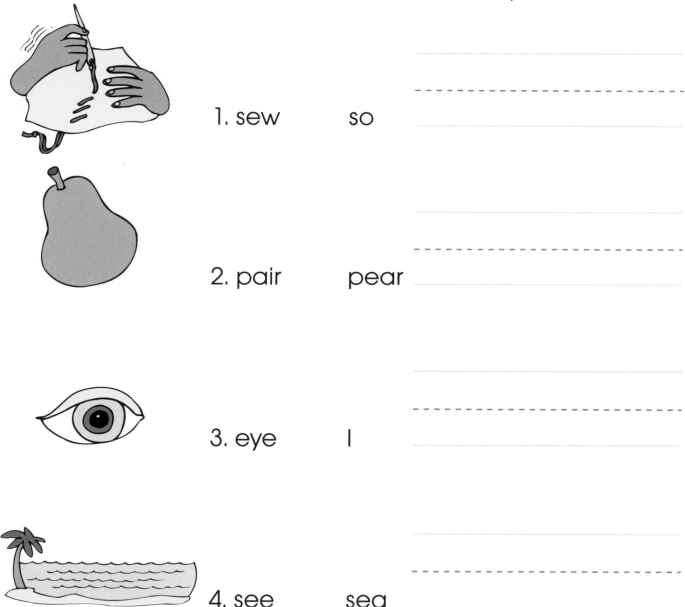

1. sew   so

2. pair   pear

3. eye   I

4. see   sea

33 *Basic Skills Helpers: Grade 1*

Telling Sentences

Directions: Read the sentences and write them below.
Begin each sentence with a capital letter.
End each sentence with a period.

1. i like to go to the store with Mom
2. we go on Friday
3. i get to push the cart
4. i get to buy the cookies
5. i like to help Mom

1. _____

2. _____

3. _____

4. _____

5. _____

34

Asking Sentences

Directions: Write the first word of each asking sentence. Be sure to begin each question with a capital letter. End each question with a question mark.

1. _____ you like the zoo   **do**

2. _____ much does it cost   **how**

3. _____ you feed the ducks   **can**

4. _____ you see the monkeys   **will**

5. _____ time will you eat lunch   **what**

Periods and Question Marks

Directions: Put a period or a question mark at the end of each sentence below.

1. Do you like parades

2. The clowns lead the parade

3. Can you hear the band

4. The balloons are big

5. Can you see the horses

Number Recognition Review

Directions: Match the correct number of objects with the number. Then match the number with the word.

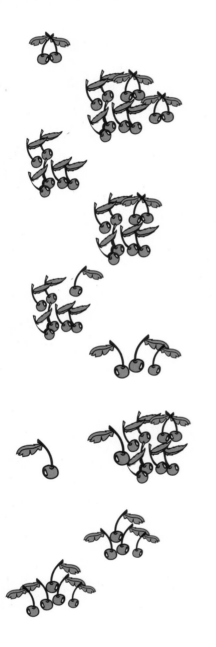

1	four
2	ten
3	two
4	six
5	one
6	nine
7	three
8	eight
9	five
10	seven

Sequencing Numbers

Sequencing is putting numbers in the correct order.

1, 2, 3, 4, 5, 6, 7, 8, 9, 10

Directions: Write the missing numbers.

Example: 4, ___5___ ,6

3, _____ ,5   7, _____ ,9   8, _____ ,10

6, _____ ,8   _____ ,3,4   _____ ,5,6

5, 6, _____   _____ ,6,7   _____ ,3,4

_____ ,4,5   _____ ,7,8   5, _____ ,7

2, 3, _____   1, 2, _____   7, 8, _____

2, _____ ,4   _____ ,2,3   4, _____ ,6

6, 7, _____   3, 4, _____   1, _____ ,3

7, 8, _____   _____ ,3,4   _____ ,9,10

Sequencing: At the Movies

Directions: The children are watching a movie. Read the sentences. Cut out the pictures below. Glue them where they belong in the picture.

1. The first child is eating popcorn.
2. The third child is eating candy.
3. The fourth child has a cup of fruit punch.
4. The second child is eating a big pretzel.

Basic Skills Helpers: Grade 1

Page is blank for cutting exercise on previous page.

Picture Problems: Addition

Directions: Solve the number problem under each picture.

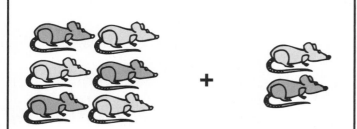

6 + 2 = _____

3 + 1 = _____

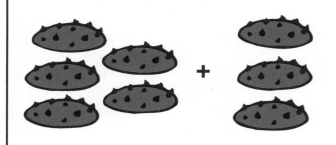

5 + 3 = _____

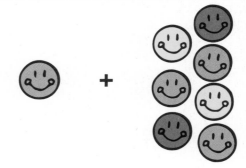

1 + 7 = _____

4 + 5 = _____

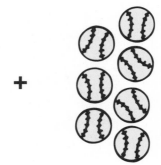

0 + 7 = _____

Picture Problems: Addition

Directions: Solve the number problem under each picture.

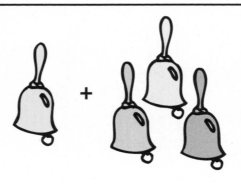

1 + 3 = _____

2 + 4 = _____

3 + 5 = _____

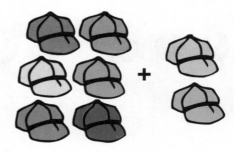

6 + 2 = _____

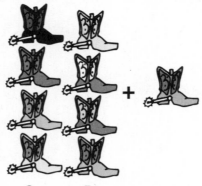

8 + 1 = _____

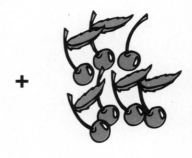

0 + 7 = _____

42

Picture Problems: Subtraction

Directions: Solve the number problem under each picture.

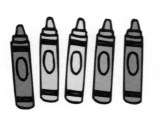 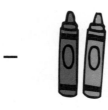

5 - 2 = _____

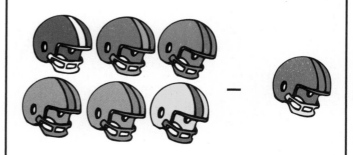

6 - 1 = _____

7 - 4 = _____

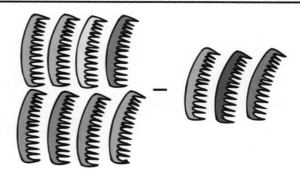

8 - 3 = _____

9 - 2 = _____

4 - 4 = _____

Basic Skills Helpers: Grade 1

Picture Problems: Subtraction

Directions: Solve the number problem under each picture.

6 - 2 = _____

9 - 5 = _____

7 - 2 = _____

4 - 1 = _____

8 - 1 = _____

4 - 0 = _____

Picture Problems: Addition and Subtraction

Directions: Solve the number problem under each picture. Write **+** or **−** to show if you should add or subtract.

How many s in all?

$7 + 5 = \underline{\quad 12 \quad}$

 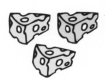

How many s are left?

$8 - 3 = \underline{\qquad}$

How many s are left?

$9 - 4 = \underline{\qquad}$

How many s in all?

$14 + 1 = \underline{\qquad}$

How many s are left?

$15 - 6 = \underline{\qquad}$

How many s in all?

$9 + 5 = \underline{\qquad}$

Addition and Subtraction

Directions: Solve the problems. Remember, addition means "putting together" or adding two or more numbers to find the sum. Subtraction means "taking away" or subtracting one number from another.

1 + 3 = _____   4 – 3 = _____   4 + 5 = _____

6 + 1 = _____   7 – 2 = _____   8 – 4 = _____

9 – 1 = _____   10 – 3 = _____

5 – 2 = _____   6 + 3 = _____

8 + 2 = _____   5 + 5 = _____

Addition and Subtraction

Remember, addition means "putting together" or adding two or more numbers to find the sum. Subtraction means "take away" or subtracting one number from another.

Directions: Solve the problems. From your answers, use the code to color the quilt.

Color:
- 6 = blue
- 7 = yellow
- 8 = green
- 9 = red
- 10 = orange

Place Value: Tens and Ones

The place value of a digit, or numeral, is shown by where it is in the number. For example, in the number **23**, **2** has the place value of **tens**, and **3** is ones.

Directions: Count the groups of ten crayons and write the number by the word **tens**. Count the other crayons and write the number by the word **ones**.

Example:

+ = __|__ ten + __|__ one

+ = ____ tens + ____ ones

+ = ____ tens + ____ ones

+ = ____ tens + ____ ones

6 tens + 3 ones = ____   5 tens + 1 one = ____

3 tens + 8 ones = ____   9 tens + 7 ones = ____

4 tens + 5 ones = ____   2 tens + 8 ones = ____

Place Value: Tens and Ones

Directions: Write the answers in the correct spaces.

		tens	ones		
3 tens, 2 ones		3	2	=	32
3 tens, 7 ones		___	___	=	___
9 tens, 1 one		___	___	=	___
5 tens, 6 ones		___	___	=	___
6 tens, 5 ones		___	___	=	___
6 tens, 8 ones		___	___	=	___
2 tens, 8 ones		___	___	=	___
4 tens, 9 ones		___	___	=	___
1 ten, 4 ones		___	___	=	___
8 tens, 2 ones		___	___	=	___
4 tens, 2 ones		___	___	=	___

28 = ____ tens, ____ ones

64 = ____ tens, ____ ones

56 = ____ tens, ____ ones

72 = ____ tens, ____ ones

38 = ____ tens, ____ ones

17 = ____ ten, ____ ones

63 = ____ tens, ____ ones

12 = ____ ten, ____ ones

Counting by Fives

Directions: Count by fives to draw the path to the playground.

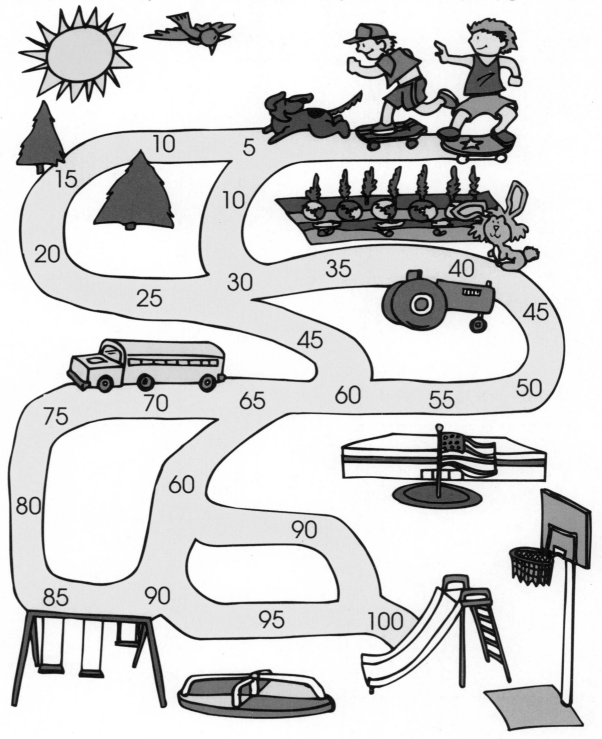

Counting by Tens

Directions: Count in order by tens to draw the path the boy takes to the store.

Basic Skills Helpers: Grade 1

Patterns: Shapes

Directions: Draw a line from the box on the left to the box on the right with the same shape and color pattern.

  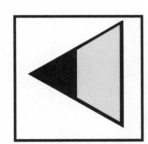 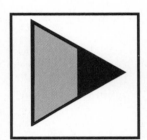

 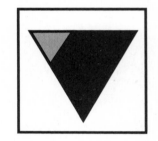  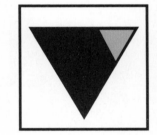

  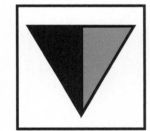 

 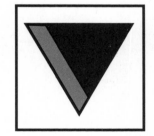  

Patterns

Directions: Draw what comes next in each pattern.

Example:

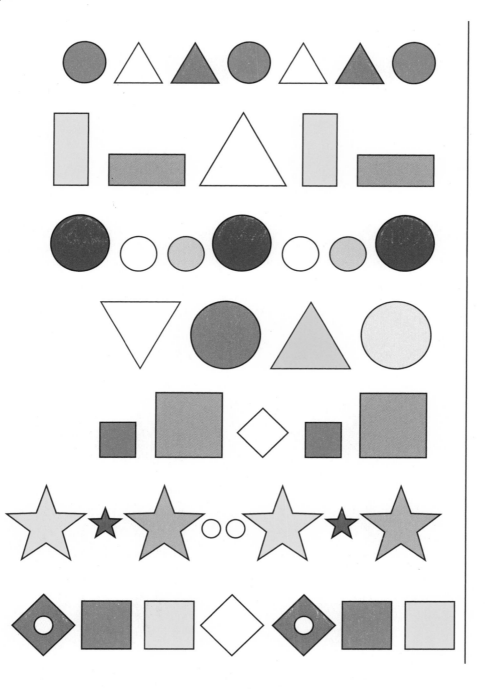

Fractions: Whole and Half

A fraction is a number that names part of a whole, such as $\frac{1}{2}$ or $\frac{3}{4}$.

Directions: Color half of each object.

Example:

Whole apple

Half an apple

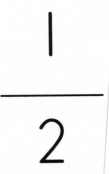

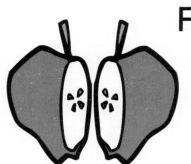

Fractions: Halves $\frac{1}{2}$

$\frac{1}{2}$ $\dfrac{\text{Part shaded or divided}}{\text{Number of equal parts}}$

Directions: Color only the shapes that show halves.

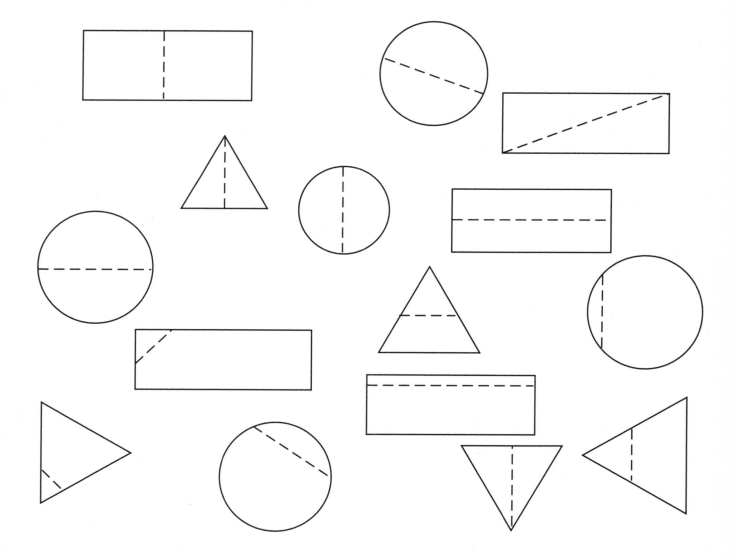

Fractions: Thirds $\frac{1}{3}$

Directions: Circle the objects that have 3 equal parts.

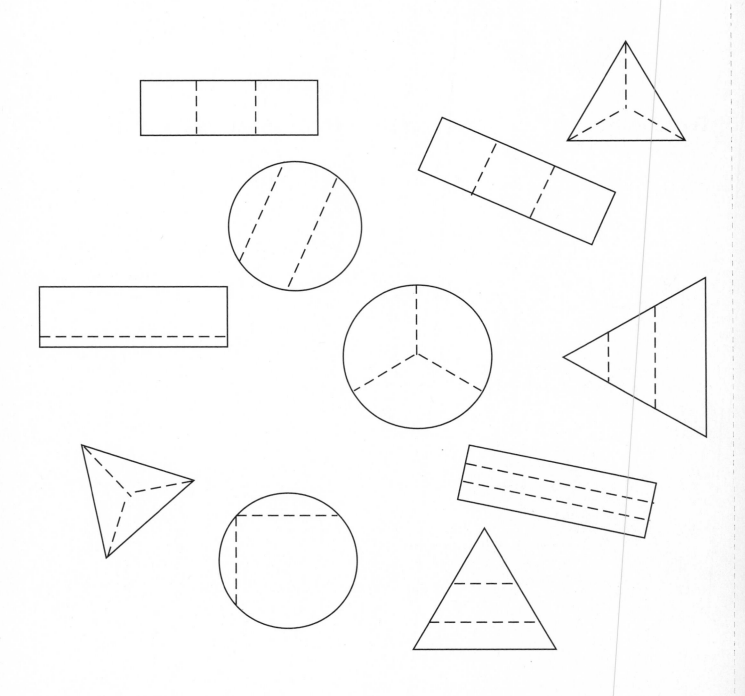

Fractions: Fourths $\frac{1}{4}$

Directions: Circle the objects that have four equal parts.

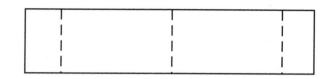

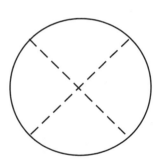
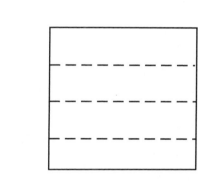
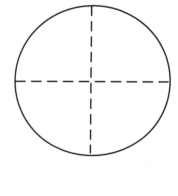

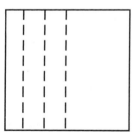
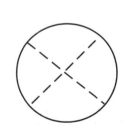
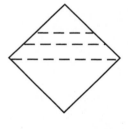

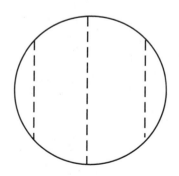
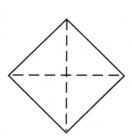
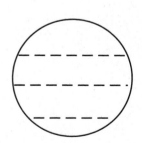

57

Review: Fractions

Directions: Count the equal parts, then write the fraction.

Example:

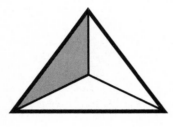

Shaded part = __1__   Write $\dfrac{1}{3}$

Equal parts = __3__

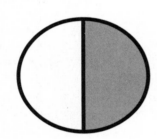

Shaded part = __1__   Write   __

Equal parts = ____

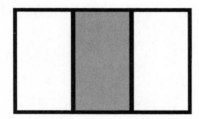

Shaded part = __1__   Write   __

Equal parts = ____

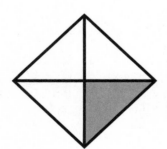

Shaded part = __1__   Write   __

Equal parts = ____

Review

Directions: Write the missing numbers by counting by tens and fives.

_____ , 20, _____ , _____ , _____ , _____ , 70, _____ , _____ , 100

5, _____ , 15, _____ , _____ , 30, _____ , _____ , _____ , _____

Directions: Color the object with thirds red. Color the object with halves blue. Color the object with fourths green.

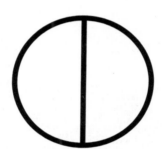 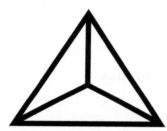 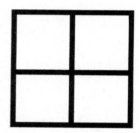

Directions: Draw a line to the correct equal part.

$\dfrac{1}{3}$

$\dfrac{1}{4}$

$\dfrac{1}{2}$

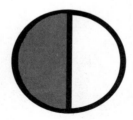

Time: Hour

The short hand of the clock tells the hour. The long hand tells how many minutes after the hour. When the minute hand is on the **12**, it is the beginning of the hour.

Directions: Look at each clock. Write the time.

Example:

___3___ o'clock

_____ o'clock

_____ o'clock

_____ o'clock

_____ o'clock

_____ o'clock

_____ o'clock

_____ o'clock

_____ o'clock

Time: Hour, Half-Hour

The short hand of the clock tells the hour. The long hand tells how many minutes after the hour. When the minute hand is on the **6**, it is on the half-hour. A half-hour is thirty minutes. It is written **:30**, such as **5:30**.

Directions: Look at each clock. Write the time.

Example:

hour   half-hour

__1__ : _30_

___ : ___   ___ : ___   ___ : ___   ___ : ___

___ : ___   ___ : ___   ___ : ___   ___ : ___

Time: Hour, Half-Hour

Directions: Draw the hands on each clock to show the correct time.

 **2:30**

 **9:00**

 **7:00**

 **4:30**

 **3:00**

 **1:30**

Review: Time

Directions: Match the time on the clock with the digital time.

$$10:00$$

$$5:00$$

$$3:00$$

$$9:00$$

$$2:00$$

Basic Skills Helpers: Grade 1

Money: Penny, Nickel, Dime

A penny is worth one cent. It is written **1¢** or **$.01**. A nickel is worth five cents. It is written **5¢** or **$.05**. A dime is worth ten cents. It is written **10¢** or **$.10**.

Directions: Add the coins pictured and write the total amounts in the blanks.

Example:

dime		**nickel**	**nickel**	**pennies**
10¢	=	5¢ +	5¢ =	10¢

10¢　　+　　1¢　　=　　_____¢　　　　10¢　　+　_____¢　=　_____¢

_____¢ +　　_____¢ +　　_____¢　　　　=　　　　_____¢

_____¢ +　　_____¢　　=　　_____¢

Money

Directions: Match the amounts in each purse to the price tags.

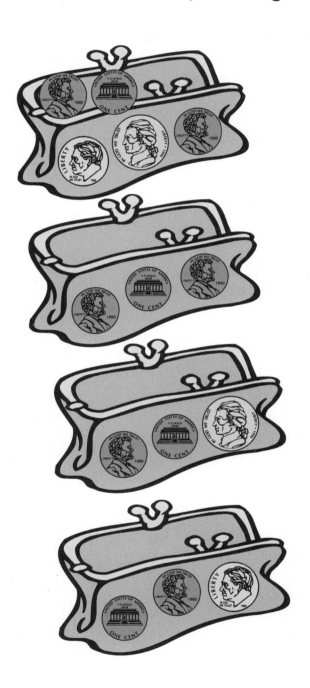

Money: Penny, Nickel, Dime

Directions: Match the correct amount of money with the price of the object.

Review

Directions: What time is it?

_____ o'clock

Directions: Draw the hands on each clock.

2:30

7:30

11:00

Directions: How much money?

= _____ ¢

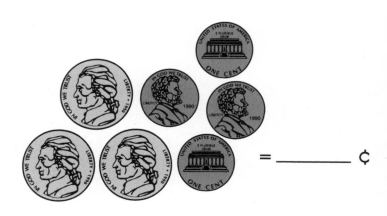
= _____ ¢

Directions: Add or subtract.

9 + 3 = _____   6 + 8 = _____   15 - 9 = _____

12 - 8 = _____   12 + 2 = _____   7 + 6 = _____

Review

Directions: Follow the instructions.

1. How much money?

_____ ¢

2.

	Tens	Ones			Hundreds	Tens	Ones
57 =	_____	_____		128 =	_____	_____	_____

3. What is this shape? Circle the answer.

Square

Triangle

Circle

What is this shape? _____

4.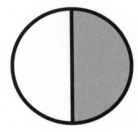

Shaded part = _____   Write ___

Equal parts = _____

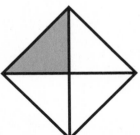

Shaded part = _____   Write

Equal parts = _____   ___

5.   12 + 3 = _____   9 + 6 = _____   15 - 7 = _____

Measurement

A ruler has 12 inches. 12 inches equal 1 foot.

Directions: Cut out the ruler at the bottom of the page. Measure the objects to the nearest inch.

The screwdriver is _____ inches long.

The pencil is _____ inches long.

The pen is _____ inches long.

The fork is _____ inches long.

_Cut ✂ _

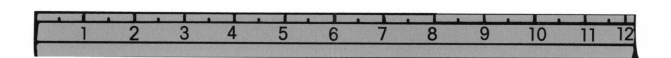

Page is blank for cutting exercise on previous page.

Answer Key

Short Vowels

Vowels are the letters **a, e, i, o** and **u**. Short **a** is the sound you hear in **ant**. Short **e** is the sound you hear in **elephant**. Short **i** is the sound you hear in **igloo**. Short **o** is the sound you hear in **octopus**. Short **u** is the sound you hear in **umbrella**.

Directions: Say the short vowel sound at the beginning of each row. Say the name of each picture. Then color the pictures which have the same short vowel sounds as that letter.

4

Short Vowel Sounds

Directions: In each box are three pictures. The words that name the pictures have missing letters. Write **a, e, i, o** or **u** to finish the words.

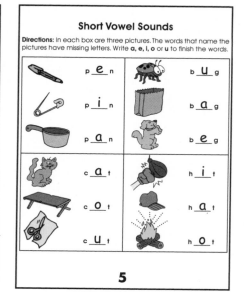

p <u>e</u> n   b <u>u</u> g
p <u>i</u> n   b <u>a</u> g
p <u>a</u> n   b <u>e</u> g
c <u>a</u> t   h <u>i</u> t
c <u>o</u> t   h <u>a</u> t
c <u>u</u> t   h <u>o</u> t

5

Long Vowels

Vowels are the letters **a, e, i, o** and **u**. Long vowel sounds say their own names. Long **a** is the sound you hear in **hay**. Long **e** is the sound you hear in **me**. Long **i** is the sound you hear in **pie**. Long **o** is the sound you hear in **no**. Long **u** is the sound you hear in **cute**.

Directions: Say the long vowel sound at the beginning of each row. Say the name of each picture. Color the pictures in each row that have the same long vowel sound as that letter.

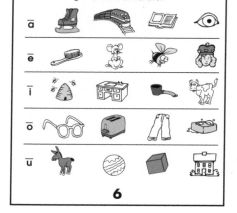

6

Long Vowel Sounds

Directions: Write **a, e, i, o** or **u** in each blank to finish the word. Draw a line from the word to the picture.

c **a** ke
r **o** se
k **i** te
f **ee** t
m **u** le

7

Consonant Blends

Consonant blends are two or more consonant sounds together in a word. The blend is made by combining the consonant sounds.

Example: floor

Directions: The name of each picture begins with a **blend**. Circle the beginning blend for each picture.

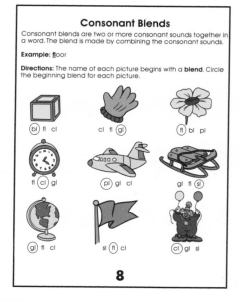

bl fl (cl)   cl fl (gl)   (fl) bl pl
fl (cl) gl   (pl) gl cl   gl fl (sl)
(gl) fl cl   sl (fl) cl   (cl) gl sl

8

Consonant Blends

Directions: The beginning blend for each word is missing. Fill in the correct blend to finish the word. Draw a line from the word to the picture.

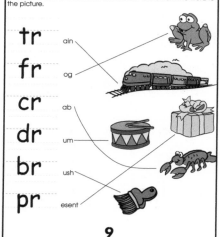

tr   ain
fr   og
cr   ab
dr   um
br   ush
pr   esent

9

Compound Words

Compound words are two words that are put together to make one new word.

Directions: Look at the pictures and the two words that are next to each other. Put the words together to make a new word. Write the new word.

Example:

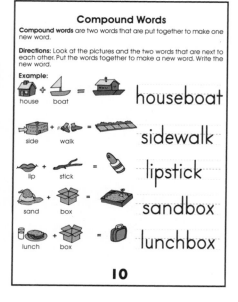

house + boat = **houseboat**
side + walk = **sidewalk**
lip + stick = **lipstick**
sand + box = **sandbox**
lunch + box = **lunchbox**

10

Basic Skills Helpers: Grade 1

Compound Words

Directions: Circle the compound word which completes each sentence. Write each word on the lines.

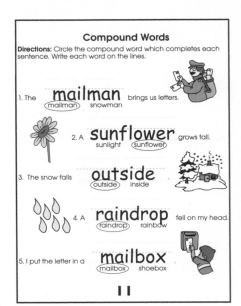

1. The **mailman** brings us letters.
   (mailman) snowman

2. A **sunflower** grows tall.
   sunlight (sunflower)

3. The snow falls **outside**
   (outside) inside

4. A **raindrop** fell on my head.
   (raindrop) rainbow

5. I put the letter in a **mailbox**
   (mailbox) shoebox

11

Riddles

Directions: Write a word from the box to answer each riddle.

| ice cream | book | chair | sun |

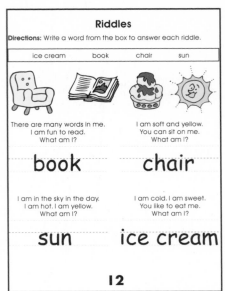

There are many words in me.
I am fun to read.
What am I?

book

I am soft and yellow.
You can sit on me.
What am I?

chair

I am in the sky in the day.
I am hot. I am yellow.
What am I?

sun

I am cold. I am sweet.
You like to eat me.
What am I?

ice cream

12

Picture Clues

Directions: Read the sentence. Circle the word that makes sense. Use the picture clues to help you. Then write the word.

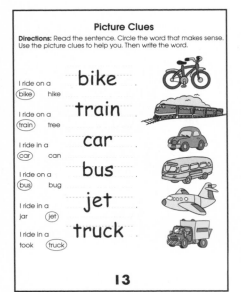

I ride on a **bike**
(bike) hike

I ride on a **train**
(train) tree

I ride in a **car**
(car) can

I ride on a **bus**
(bus) bug

I ride in a **jet**
jar (jet)

I ride in a **truck**
took (truck)

13

Comprehension

Directions: Look at the picture. Write the words from the box to finish the sentences.

| frog | log | bird | fish | ducks |

The **frog** can jump.

The turtle is on a **log**

A **bird** is in the tree.

The boy wants a **fish**

I see three **ducks**

14

Following Directions: Color the Path

Directions: Color the path the girl should take to go home. Use the sentences to help you.

1. Go to the school and turn left.
2. At the end of the street, turn right.
3. Walk past the park and turn right.
4. After you pass the pool, turn right.

15

Classifying

Directions: Classifying is sorting things into groups. Draw a circle around the pictures that answer the question.

What Can Swim?

What Can Fly?

16

Sequencing: Raking Leaves

Directions: Write a number in each box to show the order of the story.

17

Comprehension

Directions: Read the story. Write the words from the story that complete each sentence.

Jane and Bill like to play in the rain. They take off their shoes and socks.
They splash in the puddles.
It feels cold!
It is fun to splash!

Jane and Bill like to **play in the rain**

They take off their **shoes and socks**

They splash in **the puddles**

Do you like to splash in puddles? (Yes)   No

18

Comprehension: Growing Flowers

Directions: Read about flowers. Then write the answers.

Some flowers grow in pots. Many flowers grow in flower beds. Others grow beside the road. Flowers begin from seeds. They grow into small buds. Then they open wide and bloom. Flowers are pretty!

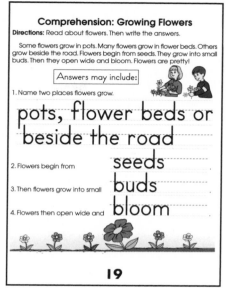

Answers may include:

1. Name two places flowers grow.

pots, flower beds or beside the road

2. Flowers begin from **seeds**

3. Then flowers grow into small **buds**

4. Flowers then open wide and **bloom**

19

Comprehension: Tigers

Directions: Read about tigers. Then write the answers.

Tigers sleep during the day. They hunt at night. Tigers eat meat. They hunt deer. They like to eat wild pigs. If they cannot find meat, tigers will eat fish.

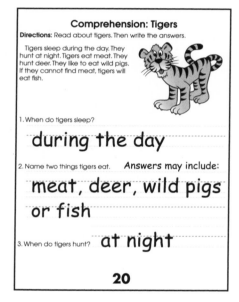

1. When do tigers sleep?

during the day

2. Name two things tigers eat.   Answers may include:

meat, deer, wild pigs or fish

3. When do tigers hunt? **at night**

20

Following Directions: Tiger Puzzle

Directions: Read the story about tigers again. Then complete the puzzle.

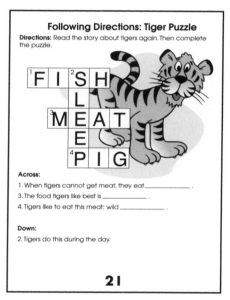

```
¹F I ²S H
    L
  ³M E A T
    E
  ⁴P I G
```

Across:

1. When tigers cannot get meat, they eat _____ .
3. The food tigers like best is _____ .
4. Tigers like to eat this meat: wild _____ .

Down:

2. Tigers do this during the day.

21

Predicting: Story Ending

Directions: Read the story. Draw a picture in the last box to complete the story.

That's my ball.   I got it first.

It's mine!   Pictures will vary.

23

Making Inferences: Feelings

Directions: Read each story. Choose a word from the box to show how each person feels.

| happy | excited | sad | mad |

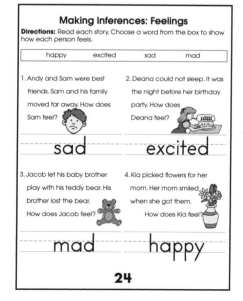

1. Andy and Sam were best friends. Sam and his family moved far away. How does Sam feel?

sad

2. Deana could not sleep. It was the night before her birthday party. How does Deana feel?

excited

3. Jacob let his baby brother play with his teddy bear. His brother lost the bear. How does Jacob feel?

mad

4. Kia picked flowers for her mom. Her mom smiled when she got them. How does Kia feel?

happy

24

Nouns

A noun is a word that names a person, place or thing. When you read a sentence, the noun is what the sentence is about.

Directions: Complete each sentence with a noun.

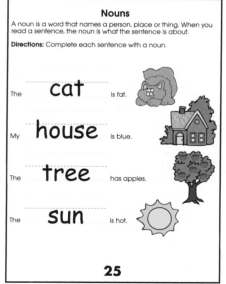

The **cat** is fat.

My **house** is blue.

The **tree** has apples.

The **sun** is hot.

25

Basic Skills Helpers: Grade 1

Nouns

Directions: Write these naming words in the correct box.

| store | zoo | child | baby | teacher | table |
| cat | park | gym | woman | sock | horse |

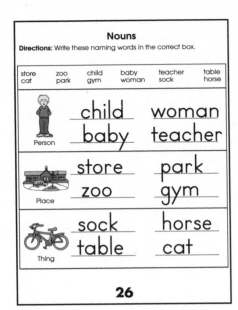

Person
child   woman
baby   teacher

Place
store   park
zoo   gym

Thing
sock   horse
table   cat

26

Verbs

Verbs are words that tell what a person or a thing can do.

Example: The girl pats the dog.
The word **pats** is the verb. It shows action.

Directions: Draw a line between the verbs and the pictures that show the action.

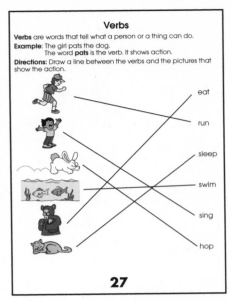

eat
run
sleep
swim
sing
hop

27

Verbs

Directions:
Look at the picture and read the words. Write an action word in each sentence below.

1. The two boys like to ___talk___ together.
2. The children ___kick___ the soccer ball.
3. Some children like to ___swing___ on the swing.
4. The girl can ___run___ very fast.
5. The teacher ___rings___ the bell.

28

Words That Describe

Describing words tell us more about a person, place or thing.

Directions: Read the words in the box. Choose the word that describes the picture. Write it next to the picture.

| happy | round | sick | cold | long |

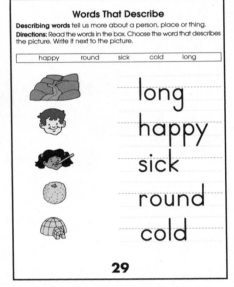

long
happy
sick
round
cold

29

Words That Describe

Directions: Circle the describing word in each sentence. Draw a line from the sentence to the picture.

1. The hungry dog is eating.
2. The tiny bird is flying.
3. Horses have long legs.
4. She is a fast runner.
5. The little boy was lost.

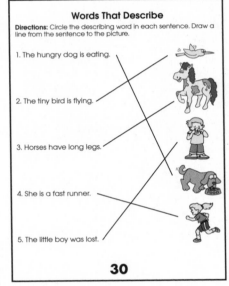

30

Synonyms

Synonyms are words that mean almost the same thing. **Start** and **begin** are synonyms.

Directions: Find the synonyms that describe each picture. Write the words in the boxes below the picture.

| small | funny | large | sad | silly | little | big | unhappy |

small
little

large
big

sad
unhappy

silly
funny

31

Antonyms

Antonyms are words that are opposites. **Hot** and **cold** are antonyms.

Directions: Draw a line between the antonyms.

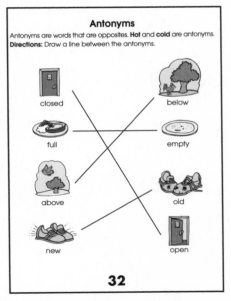

closed   below
full   empty
above   old
new   open

32

Homophones

Homophones are words that **sound** the same but are spelled differently and mean something different. **Blew** and **blue** are homophones.

Directions: Look at the word pairs. Choose the word that describes the picture. Write the word on the line next to the picture.

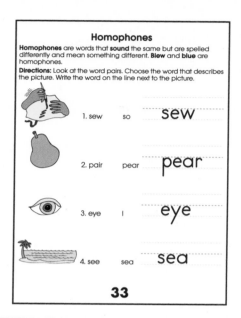

1. sew   so   sew

2. pair   pear   pear

3. eye   I   eye

4. see   sea   sea

33

Telling Sentences

Directions: Read the sentences and write them below. Begin each sentence with a capital letter. End each sentence with a period.

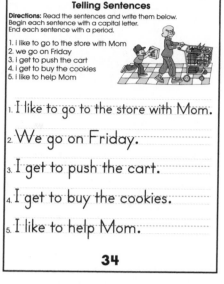

1. i like to go to the store with Mom
2. we go on Friday
3. i get to push the cart
4. i get to buy the cookies
5. I like to help Mom

1. I like to go to the store with Mom.

2. We go on Friday.

3. I get to push the cart.

4. I get to buy the cookies.

5. I like to help Mom.

34

Asking Sentences

Directions: Write the first word of each asking sentence. Be sure to begin each question with a capital letter. End each question with a question mark.

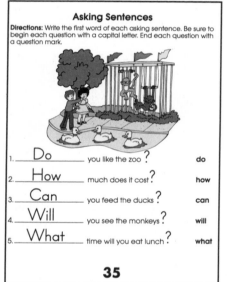

1. Do _____ you like the zoo ?   do
2. How _____ much does it cost ?   how
3. Can _____ you feed the ducks ?   can
4. Will _____ you see the monkeys ?   will
5. What _____ time will you eat lunch ?   what

35

Periods and Question Marks

Directions: Put a period or a question mark at the end of each sentence below.

1. Do you like parades ?

2. The clowns lead the parade .

3. Can you hear the band ?

4. The balloons are big .

5. Can you see the horses ?

36

Number Recognition Review

Directions: Match the correct number of objects with the number. Then match the number with the word.

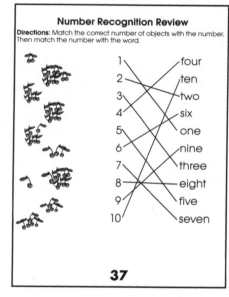

1 — four
2 — ten
3 — two
4 — six
5 — one
6 — nine
7 — three
8 — eight
9 — five
10 — seven

37

Sequencing Numbers

Sequencing is putting numbers in the correct order.
1, 2, 3, 4, 5, 6, 7, 8, 9, 10
Directions: Write the missing numbers.

Example: 4, __5__ ,6

3, __4__ ,5   7, __8__ ,9   8, __9__ ,10

6, __7__ ,8   __2__ ,3,4   __4__ ,5,6

5,6, __7__   __5__ ,6,7   __2__ ,3,4

__3__ ,4,5   __6__ ,7,8   5, __6__ ,7

2,3, __4__   1,2, __3__   7,8, __9__

2, __3__ ,4   __1__ ,2,3   4, __5__ ,6

6,7, __8__   3,4, __5__   1, __2__ ,3

7,8, __9__   __2__ ,3,4   __8__ ,9,10

38

Sequencing: At the Movies

Directions: The children are watching a movie. Read the sentences. Cut out the pictures below. Glue them where they belong in the picture.

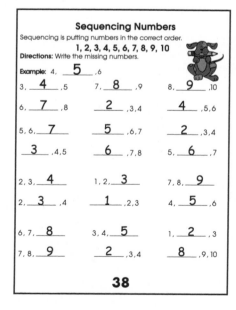

1. The first child is eating popcorn.
2. The third child is eating candy.
3. The fourth child has a cup of fruit punch.
4. The second child is eating a big pretzel.

39

Basic Skills Helpers: Grade 1

Picture Problems: Addition
Directions: Solve the number problem under each picture.

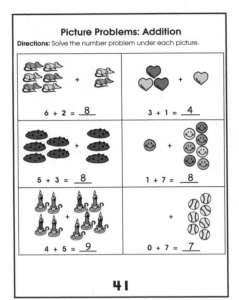

6 + 2 = 8   3 + 1 = 4

5 + 3 = 8   1 + 7 = 8

4 + 5 = 9   0 + 7 = 7

41

Picture Problems: Addition
Directions: Solve the number problem under each picture.

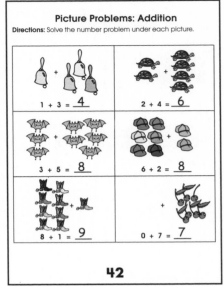

1 + 3 = 4   2 + 4 = 6

3 + 5 = 8   6 + 2 = 8

8 + 1 = 9   0 + 7 = 7

42

Picture Problems: Subtraction
Directions: Solve the number problem under each picture.

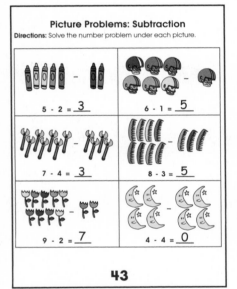

5 - 2 = 3   6 - 1 = 5

7 - 4 = 3   8 - 3 = 5

9 - 2 = 7   4 - 4 = 0

43

Picture Problems: Subtraction
Directions: Solve the number problem under each picture.

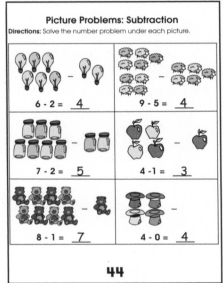

6 - 2 = 4   9 - 5 = 4

7 - 2 = 5   4 - 1 = 3

8 - 1 = 7   4 - 0 = 4

44

Picture Problems: Addition and Subtraction
Directions: Solve the number problem under each picture.
Write + or – to show if you should add or subtract.

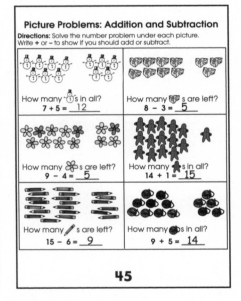

How many ☃'s in all?
7 + 5 = 12

How many 🐺 s are left?
8 – 3 = 5

How many 🌼 s are left?
9 – 4 = 5

How many ★ s in all?
14 + 1 = 15

How many ✏ s are left?
15 – 6 = 9

How many ☕ s in all?
9 + 5 = 14

45

Addition and Subtraction
Directions: Solve the problems. Remember, addition means "putting together" or adding two or more numbers to find the sum. Subtraction means "taking away" or subtracting one number from another.

1 + 3 = 4   4 - 3 = 1   4 + 5 = 9

6 + 1 = 7   7 - 2 = 5   8 - 4 = 4

9 - 1 = 8   10 - 3 = 7

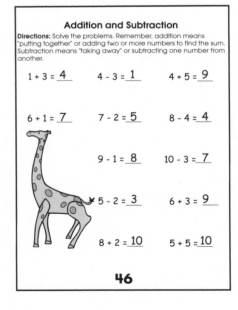

5 - 2 = 3   6 + 3 = 9

8 + 2 = 10   5 + 5 = 10

46

Addition and Subtraction
Remember, addition means "putting together" or adding two or more numbers to find the sum. Subtraction means "take away" or subtracting one number from another.

Directions: Solve the problems. From your answers, use the code to color the quilt.

Color:
6 = blue
7 = yellow
8 = green
9 = red
10 = orange

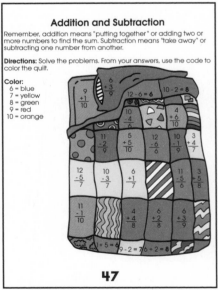

47

Place Value: Tens and Ones

The place value of a digit, or numeral, is shown by where it is in the number. For example, in the number **23**, **2** has the place value of **tens**, and **3** is ones.

Directions: Count the groups of ten crayons and write the number by the word **tens**. Count the other crayons and write the number by the word **ones**.

Example:

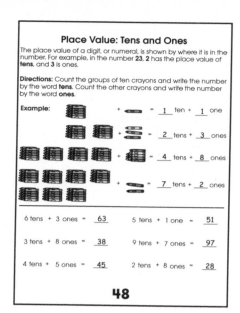

+ = _1_ ten + _1_ one

+ = _2_ tens + _3_ ones

+ = _4_ tens + _8_ ones

+ = _7_ tens + _2_ ones

6 tens + 3 ones = _63_		5 tens + 1 one = _51_
3 tens + 8 ones = _38_		9 tens + 7 ones = _97_
4 tens + 5 ones = _45_		2 tens + 8 ones = _28_

48

Place Value: Tens and Ones

Directions: Write the answers in the correct spaces.

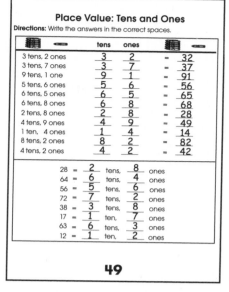

	tens	ones		
3 tens, 2 ones	3	2	=	32
3 tens, 7 ones	3	7	=	37
9 tens, 1 one	9	1	=	91
5 tens, 6 ones	5	6	=	56
6 tens, 5 ones	6	5	=	65
6 tens, 8 ones	6	8	=	68
2 tens, 8 ones	2	8	=	28
4 tens, 9 ones	4	9	=	49
1 ten, 4 ones	1	4	=	14
8 tens, 2 ones	8	2	=	82
4 tens, 2 ones	4	2	=	42

28	=	_2_	tens,	_8_	ones
64	=	_6_	tens,	_4_	ones
56	=	_5_	tens,	_6_	ones
72	=	_7_	tens,	_2_	ones
38	=	_3_	tens,	_8_	ones
17	=	_1_	ten,	_7_	ones
63	=	_6_	tens,	_3_	ones
12	=	_1_	ten,	_2_	ones

49

Counting by Fives

Directions: Count by fives to draw the path to the playground.

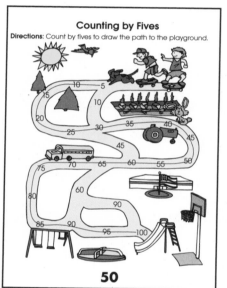

50

Counting by Tens

Directions: Count in order by tens to draw the path the boy takes to the store.

51

Patterns: Shapes

Directions: Draw a line from the box on the left to the box on the right with the same shape and color pattern.

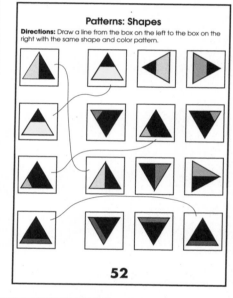

52

Patterns

Directions: Draw what comes next in each pattern.

Example:

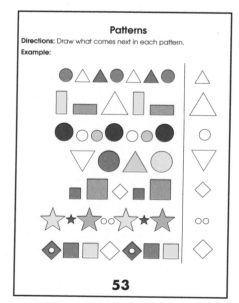

53

Fractions: Whole and Half

A fraction is a number that names part of a whole, such as $\frac{1}{2}$ or $\frac{3}{4}$.

Directions: Color half of each object.

Example:

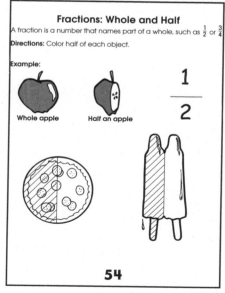

Whole apple   Half an apple

$$\frac{1}{2}$$

54

Basic Skills Helpers: Grade 1

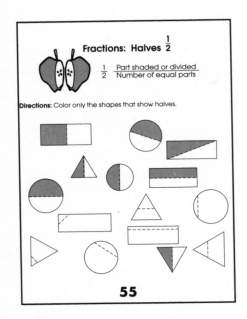

Fractions: Halves $\frac{1}{2}$

$\frac{1}{2}$ | Part shaded or divided
--- | Number of equal parts

Directions: Color only the shapes that show halves.

55

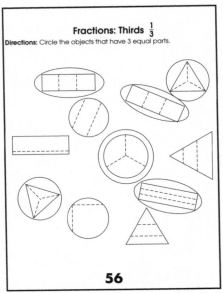

Fractions: Thirds $\frac{1}{3}$

Directions: Circle the objects that have 3 equal parts.

56

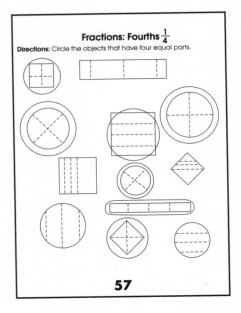

Fractions: Fourths $\frac{1}{4}$

Directions: Circle the objects that have four equal parts.

57

Review: Fractions

Directions: Count the equal parts, then write the fraction.

Example:

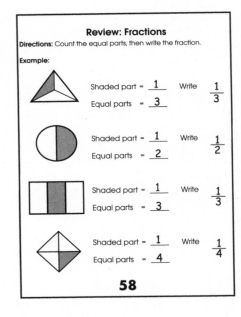

Shaded part = 1   Write $\frac{1}{3}$
Equal parts = 3

Shaded part = 1   Write $\frac{1}{2}$
Equal parts = 2

Shaded part = 1   Write $\frac{1}{3}$
Equal parts = 3

Shaded part = 1   Write $\frac{1}{4}$
Equal parts = 4

58

Review

Directions: Write the missing numbers by counting by tens and fives.

10 , 20, 30 , 40 , 50 , 60 , 70, 80 , 90 , 100

5, 10 , 15, 20 , 25 , 30, 35 , 40 , 45 , 50

Directions: Color the object with thirds red. Color the object with halves blue. Color the object with fourths green.

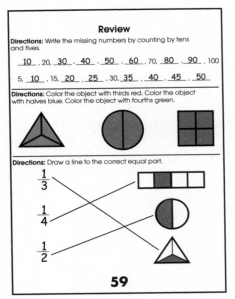

Directions: Draw a line to the correct equal part.

$\frac{1}{3}$

$\frac{1}{4}$

$\frac{1}{2}$

59

Time: Hour

The short hand of the clock tells the hour. The long hand tells how many minutes after the hour. When the minute hand is on the **12**, it is the beginning of the hour.

Directions: Look at each clock. Write the time.

Example:

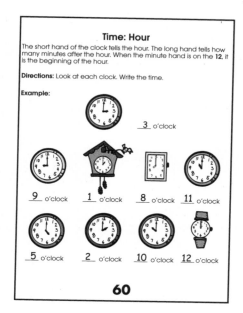

_3_ o'clock

_9_ o'clock _1_ o'clock _8_ o'clock _11_ o'clock

_5_ o'clock _2_ o'clock _10_ o'clock _12_ o'clock

60

Time: Hour, Half-Hour

The short hand of the clock tells the hour. The long hand tells how many minutes after the hour. When the minute hand is on the **6**, it is on the half-hour. A half-hour is thirty minutes. It is written **:30**, such as **5:30**.

Directions: Look at each clock. Write the time.

Example:

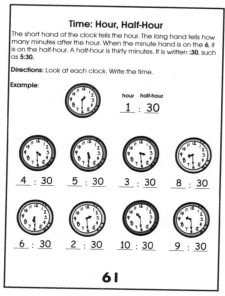

hour half-hour
_1_ : _30_

_4_ : _30_ _5_ : _30_ _3_ : _30_ _8_ : _30_

_6_ : _30_ _2_ : _30_ _10_ : _30_ _9_ : _30_

61

Time: Hour, Half-Hour

Directions: Draw the hands on each clock to show the correct time.

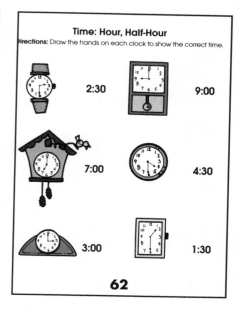

2:30   9:00

7:00   4:30

3:00   1:30

62

Review: Time

Directions: Match the time on the clock with the digital time.

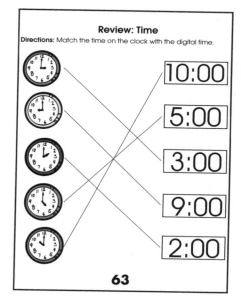

10:00

5:00

3:00

9:00

2:00

63

Money: Penny, Nickel, Dime

A penny is worth one cent. It is written **1¢** or **$.01**. A nickel is worth five cents. It is written **5¢** or **$.05**. A dime is worth ten cents. It is written **10¢** or **$.10**.

Directions: Add the coins pictured and write the total amounts in the blanks.

Example:

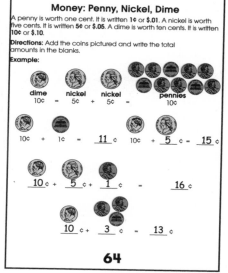

dime   nickel   nickel   pennies
10¢ = 5¢ + 5¢ =   10¢

10¢ + 1¢ = _11_ ¢   10¢ + _5_ ¢ = _15_ ¢

_10_ ¢ + _5_ ¢ + _1_ ¢ = _16_ ¢

_10_ ¢ + _3_ ¢ = _13_ ¢

64

         Basic Skills Helpers: Grade 1

Money

Directions: Match the amounts in the purse to the price tags.

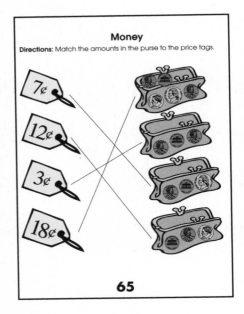

Money: Penny, Nickel, Dime

Directions: Match the correct amount of money with the price of the object.

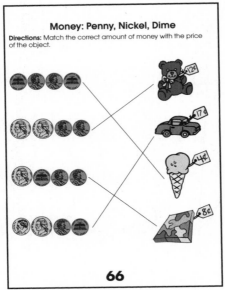

Review

Directions: What time is it?

___3___ o'clock

Directions: Draw the hands on each clock.

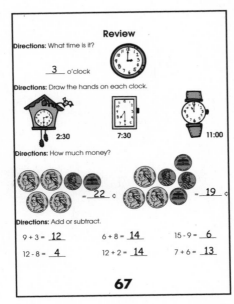

2:30   7:30   11:00

Directions: How much money?

= __22__ ¢   = __19__ ¢

Directions: Add or subtract.

9 + 3 = __12__   6 + 8 = __14__   15 - 9 = __6__

12 - 8 = __4__   12 + 2 = __14__   7 + 6 = __13__

65

66

67

Review

Directions: Follow the instructions.
1. How much money?

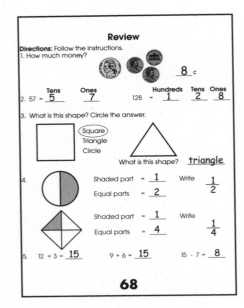

__8__ ¢

2. 57 = | **Tens** | **Ones** | 128 = | **Hundreds** | **Tens** | **Ones** |

2. 57 = __5__ Tens __7__ Ones   128 = __1__ Hundreds __2__ Tens __8__ Ones

3. What is this shape? Circle the answer.

(Square)
Triangle
Circle

What is this shape? __triangle__

4. Shaded part = __1__   Write __1/2__
    Equal parts = __2__

    Shaded part = __1__   Write __1/4__
    Equal parts = __4__

5. 12 + 3 = __15__   9 + 6 = __15__   15 - 7 = __8__

68

Measurement

A ruler has 12 inches. 12 inches equal 1 foot.

Directions: Cut out the ruler at the bottom of the page. Measure the objects to the nearest inch.

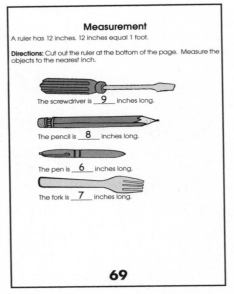

The screwdriver is __9__ inches long.

The pencil is __8__ inches long.

The pen is __6__ inches long.

The fork is __7__ inches long.

69